Kidz Biz

BOOK 1

Recycling: Earning Money While Saving Our Planet

Gwen Richardson

KIDZ BIZ: BOOK 1

FIRST EDITION
Cover design by Zeeshan Tahir

ISBN: 9781693627729
10 9 8 7 6 5 4 3 2 1
Printed in the United States of America

Facebook: @kidzbizsquad
Email: gwenrichardson123@gmail.com
Website: www.gwenrichardson.com

To the children who are
the future entrepreneurs around the world

Daisy walked outside to see if either of her friends, Robert or Karim, were playing. School was out for the summer, and Daisy was eager to see if they had any plans for the day. Her parents did not want her to stay cooped up in her room playing video games all summer. "You need to get some fresh air and play outside with your friends like we did when we were growing up," her mother said.

Daisy saw Karim riding his skateboard and waved for him to come over. "Hi, Daisy," said Karim. "What are you doing?"

"Nothing yet," replied Daisy, who had recently celebrated her tenth birthday. "Have you seen Robert today?"

"No," said Karim, "but he called me this morning and said he would be coming outside at about 10 o'clock."

"When he comes outside, I have something I want the two of you to help me do," said Daisy.

"What's that?" asked Karim.

"There is an American Girl doll™ I want, but my parents said it costs too much," said Daisy. "My birthday already passed, and it's not close to Christmas, so they said I can't have it right now. But if I can earn half of the money to buy it, they said they would match the other half and get it for me."

"I thought you didn't like to play with dolls," said Karim, who knew that Daisy was a math whiz who also enjoyed playing with all sorts of devices.

"I usually don't," said Daisy, "but this doll is special. It's a one-of-a-kind doll that no one else will have. Even when I grow up, it will still be special to me."

"How much does it cost?" asked nine-year-old Karim.

"It costs $200," replied Daisy.

"Wow!"

Just then, Robert ran toward them.

"Wow what?" asked Robert, curious about what Daisy and Karim were discussing.

"Daisy wants a doll that costs $200," said Karim.

"Are your parents going to buy it?" asked Robert.

"Only if I can earn half of the money. Half of $200 is $100," Daisy replied.

Daisy hoped they would help. "Can you guys help me think of a way to earn the money?"

Robert and Karim were quiet for a few seconds, trying to think of ways the three of them could earn money.

"I think I have an idea," said Robert. "I was watching TV the other day, and there was a news story about a man who picked up soda cans off the street for three months and made almost one thousand dollars."

"That's a lot of money," said Karim. "That's a lot more than Daisy needs. Maybe if we help her for the next few weeks, she will have enough. Robert, how much did the man get paid for each can?"

"On the news report, it said he was paid five cents per can," Robert replied.

"Let's see," said Daisy. "According to my calculations, at five cents per can, it will take 2,000 cans for me to raise $100," she said, showing off her math skills.

"Wow! That's a lot of cans," Karim exclaimed. "But I'm sure, with the three of us working together, we can do it in no time."

Daisy was excited. "Thank you for your idea, Robert, and thank you both for helping me to earn the money to buy my very own American Girl doll™."

"Now I have to ask my parents if it's okay for us to collect the cans, and we need somewhere to store them until we have enough," she said. "I also need to ask them to find out where to take them for recycling."

"We will be helping Daisy and keeping our neighborhood clean at the same time," said Karim. "Let's meet here about this time tomorrow once Daisy has had a chance to talk with her parents."

Daisy went home, but she waited until her father came home from work that evening before asking them about the recycling. Daisy's mother was a middle school teacher, and she had summers off.

After her father got home and they had eaten dinner, Daisy said, "Mom and Dad, I have something to ask you. Remember when you said I could have an American Girl doll™ if I could earn half the money? I was talking with Robert and Karim today, and we came up with an idea."

"What's the idea, Daisy?" her father asked as her mother listened.

"I can collect aluminum cans we use, ask our neighbors to give us theirs, and maybe ask the owner of the corner store if he has some I can have. Robert and Karim have said they would help me until I have enough money saved," Daisy said.

"That sounds like it will require a lot of cans. How long do you think it will take?" asked Daisy's mother.

"I hope we have enough cans at the end of three to four weeks. But even if it takes longer, it will be worth it," Daisy replied.

Her parents looked at each other and smiled. "We are very proud of you for thinking of a creative solution to your problem. We will help you in any way we can."

"Thanks so much, Mom and Dad," said Daisy. "All I need from you is a place to store the cans while we are collecting them. I will also need you to find a company that will recycle them and will pay five cents per can. If I think of anything else, I will let you know."

"You have our permission to ask our neighbors on this street and the next street over, Daisy," said her mother. "But if you want to go anywhere else, I'll need to take you in the car or walk with you so you will be safe."

"Thank you so much," said Daisy as she hugged both of her parents.

The next day, she met Robert and Karim and told them the good news. "My parents said yes to the recycling idea, and they also said they would help with storing the cans," said Daisy.

"Great," said Robert and Karim. "Why don't we get started right away?" declared Karim. "We can go to each neighbor's house and ask them for cans, and we can use my wagon to put the cans in to make it easy to move them."

Karim went home to get his red wagon, and the three of them started going door to door asking for soda cans. They also asked their neighbors if they would save cans for them and told them they would stop by later to pick them up. By the end of the first day, they had already collected 100 cans.

"If we collect 100 cans each day, it will only take us 20 days to get 2,000 cans total," Daisy calculated.

"We probably won't be able to do this every single day," said Robert. "But even if it takes us 30 days, that's about a month from now, and you'll be able to order your American Girl doll™."

"You are right, Robert, especially since we have to go to church on Sundays and Karim takes swimming lessons twice a week," Daisy said. "But that is still exciting because I never thought I would be able to get the doll. You guys are awesome!"

Over the next few weeks, Daisy, Robert, and Karim faithfully collected cans. Daisy even visited a couple of grocery stores and asked the managers if they would give her their discarded cans. The managers were more than happy to help.

Since they stored the cans in two tall, plastic trash cans that filled up fast, Daisy and her parents decided to go to the recycling plant once a week to deliver the cans and collect the recycling fee. After only five weeks, Daisy had earned $104.15!

Daisy and her parents went to the American Girl doll™ website and ordered the custom-made doll. Her package arrived three weeks later, and Daisy was grinning from ear to ear. Shortly after that, she called Robert and Karim and invited them over to her house to see it.

"Dolls are mostly for girls," said Robert, "but I understand why you wanted it."

"Yes, the doll is beautiful," Karim said.

"I couldn't have done it without the two of you," Daisy said. "If either of you ever want my help to earn money for a cool toy or device, just let me know. I'll be happy to help. With three people working together, it is much easier to achieve any goal."

The End

ABOUT THE AUTHOR

Gwen Richardson is a long-time entrepreneur with a passion to plant the seed of entrepreneurship in the next generation. Each installment in the Kidz Biz book series will cover a different business concept or aspect of running a business.

A graduate of Georgetown University, Ms. Richardson currently resides in Houston, Texas.

Communication via email is welcome, including speaking requests. Email the author at gwenrichardson123@gmail.com.

Visit the author's website: www.gwenrichardson.com

Facebook: @kidzbizsquad

Made in the USA
Monee, IL
25 August 2020